Lola's Parol

Lola's Parol

by Nuelma P. Legaspi
illustrations by Hannah R. Licudine

To my beautiful Lola Paulita:

I miss you very much.

"God be with you.
Take care, drive safely,
go home happy.
And remember:
we love you very,
very much."

–Lola Paulita

She is a bright parol, a star.
Her belly laughs can be heard from afar.

Her warmth guides my way,
her touch takes pain away.

She is made with love
and gratitude, always, for up above.

She helps me when I trip and fall,
gives me vapor rub and rubbing alcohol.

She stands by me when times are rough,
believes in my best, tells me I'm enough.

She smells of roses and sampaguita.
We call her, the Beautiful Lola Ita.

She listens and offers advice
while frying fish and cooking rice.

Always surrounded by
family and friends,

she loved deeply
'til the end.

But time with her will cease.
The brightness will one day decrease.

And then the world becomes dark.
No more scent, no more touch, no warm spark.

It feels lonely and cold.
I just want her back to hold.

I must remember: when she left me,
it took away her pain and set her free.

In time, I grow to accept
only memories are left.

These memories, they spark light.
And once again, the parol takes flight.

Her love will never part.
The legacy she left brings joy to my heart.

Life with her has been my greatest reward
and the peace within me is being restored.

My heart, it is whole.
I will always love her, my Lola, my Parol.

In remembrance of loved ones lost,
but never forgotten.

May this book bring you
peace and comfort.

Acknowledgments

Thank you to the incredible team who helped make my vision a reality: Johna, my editor, Hannah, my illustrator, and Jodi, my book designer. The support and love you've given this book is more than I could have asked for. You all are so talented and I'm forever grateful.

To my loving husband, Ed: thank you for always believing in me even through my doubts, the unconditional love you show for nothing in return, and the continuous support you give to me in everything I do. You make my life complete. I love you.

About the Author

Nuelma "Amy" Patio Legaspi is a Filipino American who works in the medical technology industry. She enjoys spending quality time with her husband, Ed, and their sons, Jacob (8) and Jasper (5); traveling; and learning and creating new things, whether that's opening a small business or authoring a children's book.

With her newfound love for creative writing, Amy wants to create books that introduce and share Filipino culture in a fun way with her US-raised kids, while also giving them a way to grieve the loss of their great-grandmother. She hopes to feature more Asian American culture in her writing.

About this book:

Lola's Parol by Nuelma P. Legaspi
Published by Nuelma P. Legaspi

www.nuelmalegaspibooks.com

Book design by Jodi Giddings

ISBN: 978-0-578-99232-7

First Edition

Made in the USA
Las Vegas, NV
24 November 2021